JAN 2 7 1992	DATE DUE	
MAY 2 5 1992 / NOV 2 1 1994		
APR 0 6 1993		
MAY 1 3 1993 / APR 1 5 1995 / JUL 1 0 1995		
Apr 15, 94 / AUG 1 4 '95		
MAY 1 8 1994 / SEP 1 9 1995		
AUG 2 4 1994		
SEP 0 6 1994 / JAN 2 0 1996		
SEP 2 7 1994 / JUN 0 1 1996		
OCT 1 8 1994		
DEC 1 7 1994		

Smith, Alexander McCall.
    The ice-cream bicycle / Alexander McCall Smith ;
illustrated by Stephanie Ryder. -- London : Viking,
1990.
    79 p. : ill. -- (Read alone)

04490843   ISBN:0670830771

I. Ryder, Stephanie. II. Title

1016   91MAR01   36/mc   1-00544627

MAR 1 3 1991

 *Get set with Read Alone!*

This entertaining series is designed for all new readers who want to start reading a whole book on their own.

The stories are lively and fun, with lots of illustrations and clear, large type, to make first solo reading a perfect pleasure!

Some other titles in the series

DODIE Finola Akister
SIMON'S MAGIC BOBBLE HAT Bill Bevan
GERBIL CRAZY Tony Bradman
THE SLIPPERS THAT TALKED
  Gyles Brandreth
FAT PUSS AND FRIENDS Harriet Castor
FAT PUSS ON WHEELS Harriet Castor
POOR LITTLE MARY Kathryn Cave
FINDERS KEEPERS June Crebbin
DRAGON RIDE Helen Cresswell
HELP! Margaret Gordon
WILLIE WHISKERS Margaret Gordon

Alexander McCall Smith

The Ice-Cream Bicycle

Illustrated by Stephanie Ryder

VIKING

VIKING

Published by the Penguin Group
27 Wrights Lane, London W8 5TZ, England
Viking Penguin Inc., 40 West 23rd Street, New York, New York 10010, USA
Penguin Books Australia Ltd, Ringwood, Victoria, Australia
Penguin Books Canada Ltd, 2801 John Street, Markham, Ontario, Canada L3R 1B4
Penguin Books (NZ) Ltd, 182–190 Wairau Road, Auckland 10, New Zealand

Penguin Books Ltd, Registered Offices: Harmondsworth, Middlesex, England

First published 1990
10 9 8 7 6 5 4 3 2 1

Filmset in 18/24pt Linotron 202 Times by
Rowland Phototypesetting (London) Ltd
Printed in Great Britain by
Butler and Tanner Ltd, Frome and London

A CIP catalogue record for this book is available from the British Library

ISBN 0–670–83077–1

Chapter One

There were many bicycles in Misipo's town, but not one of them was as special as the ice-cream bicycle. This bicycle, which was painted white all over, had a large metal box fixed above the front wheel. The box was rather like a fridge. When a block of ice was put in it and the top was

closed, ice-cream could be kept cool inside. Then the bicycle could be pedalled to wherever there were people who might like to buy ice-cream. There were plenty of such people, because the town was in Africa and in the hot season people often longed for something to keep them cool.

The ice-cream bicycle belonged to Misipo's uncle, who lived in a small room at the back of Misipo's house. He was a cheerful man, who liked to play football with his nephews, and who could always be heard whistling some

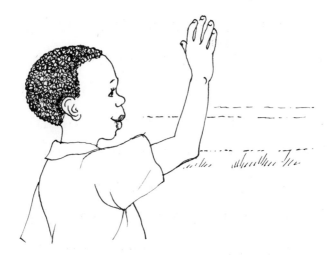

tune or other under his breath.
Every morning, Uncle would
wheel the bicycle out of its
shed, check that the tyres were
pumped up, and set off, waving
to Misipo as he went on his way.

"It would be fun to go with
your uncle one day, wouldn't
it?" Misipo's friend Sepo once
said. "Couldn't you ask him?"

Misipo thought for a
moment. Now that Sepo had
made the suggestion, it seemed
a very good idea.

That evening, when Uncle
came home from his rounds,
Misipo asked whether he and
his friend could go with him
when he went out to sell his ice-
creams on Saturday. Saturday

was always a busy day for ice-
cream sellers, and Misipo
thought that he and Sepo
might be able to help.

Uncle smiled.

"But I can't take you both
on the bicycle," he said. "I
could carry one, but not two.

Wait, I have an idea. One can run behind while the other rides with me. And then you can change places."

Now that Uncle had agreed to the plan, Misipo ran off to Sepo's house to tell him the good news. Sepo was delighted.

"I can't wait for Saturday,"
he said. "Can you?"

"No," said Misipo. "I can't
wait either."

They had to wait, of course, but at last Saturday morning arrived and the two boys were standing outside the house while Uncle wheeled the bicycle out of its shed.

"The first thing we have to do," he explained, "is to go to the factory. That's where we buy the blocks of ice and the ice-creams themselves. You boys can help me load them."

"And then what happens?" Misipo asked.

"We start on our rounds," said Uncle. "We'll begin in the middle of town. There are always lots of shoppers about on a Saturday morning. They usually enjoy an ice-cream after doing their shopping."

Sepo was the first to ride on the bicycle. Perched on the crossbar, he hung firmly on to the handlebars to keep himself from falling off. Then Uncle

mounted the saddle, called out to Misipo, and the three of them set off.

Uncle did not pedal fast, and so Misipo found it quite easy to trot along beside them. Every so often Uncle would give a ring on the great silver bell on the handlebars. This was not

for any special reason, he said,
but purely because it was
Saturday and he was in a
happy mood.

After ten minutes it was
Misipo's turn to ride on the
bicycle. They were now very
near the factory, and so it was
not long before he had to jump
off and help stack the blocks of

ice and the ice-creams. Then
they set off again, the bicycle
going even slower now because
of its heavy, but delicious, load.

They found a shady place near
the centre of town, and within
a few minutes the first
customers arrived. Most of
them chatted happily with
Uncle and laughed at his jokes.
Misipo and Sepo helped to get
the ice-creams out of the box
and to tidy up the sticky papers
afterwards. By lunch-time they
had sold over half the ice-
creams and Uncle suggested
that they should go and wait

outside the railway station.

"There's a big train due in," he said, "and there'll be plenty of people wanting to buy ice-creams."

They parked under a palm tree just outside the railway station. As Uncle had predicted, the ice-creams sold quickly. Soon there were just two or three ice-creams left, and before long these, too, were gone.

"That's it," said Uncle, smiling with pleasure. "That's business over for the day."

The boys were disappointed. They had enjoyed themselves

so much that they would have been quite happy to continue selling ice-creams. Now all the excitement was over and they would have to return home.

"I still have something to do before we go," said Uncle. "I have to see a man in that store over there. I'll just be ten

minutes or so. You two stay here and look after the bicycle."

Uncle crossed the road, leaving the two boys sitting under the palm tree. They watched the people who were still coming out of the railway station. Many of them had

travelled long distances, and were carrying all sorts of baggage. It was an exciting place to be.

Suddenly there came a loud whistle from within the station.

"That'll be a train about to leave," said Sepo.

"Should we go and watch it?" Misipo asked. "Just for a minute?"

"Yes," said Sepo. "We can come straight back."

Chapter Two

The boys were just in time to
see the train pull out of the
station. They stood on the
platform for a few minutes,
watching the great steam-
engine puff and hiss as it began
its journey. They watched the
coaches go past, crammed full
of waving passengers, and
then, as the platform suddenly

became quiet again, they made their way back to their place under the palm tree.

Sepo was the first to notice what had happened.

"The bicycle!" he blurted out. "It's not there!"

Misipo's heart sank. Followed by his friend, he ran to the place where they had left the bicycle and looked around. It was nowhere to be seen.

"Perhaps your uncle's taken it home," said Sepo. "Perhaps he came back early and was cross because we weren't there."

Misipo would have liked to

believe this, but he knew that it was probably not true.

"It's been stolen," he said to his friend. "We shouldn't have left it."

Sepo said nothing. He had just seen Uncle come out of the store on the other side of the street. Uncle was smiling, but, as he approached the boys and saw that the bicycle was not there, the smile was replaced by a look of concern.

"Where's the bicycle?" he asked the boys. "Has something happened?"

As they made their way to the police station, Misipo tried

to tell Uncle how sorry he was.

"We were only gone for a moment," he said. "We didn't think that anybody would take it."

Uncle said nothing.

"I'm very sorry, Uncle," Misipo continued. "I didn't think . . ."

"Don't talk about it any more," said Uncle. "Anybody can make a mistake like that."

Misipo had never seen his Uncle get cross before and, even now, Uncle was hiding his anger. He knew, though, how serious things were. Uncle made his living with the ice-

cream bicycle, and without it
he would have no job. And all
of this was the fault of Sepo
and himself. It was almost too
much to think about.

At the police station, the
policeman listened carefully as
Uncle told him what had
happened. He wanted to know

exactly what the bike looked like and wrote down a long description of the bicycle in a large book. Then, when this was done, he closed the book, and put it away on a shelf.

"Do you think you'll be able to find it?" Uncle asked. "Will it take you long?"

The policeman shook his head.

"This is a big town," he said. "There are hundreds of bicycles stolen. It happens all the time."

Uncle was silent for a few moments.

"So it might be quite a few

days," he said at last. "Maybe even a week or so?"

The policeman looked at him sadly.

"If I were you," he said, "I'd forget about that bicycle."

Misipo could hardly believe what he heard. What was the point of having policemen if they couldn't even find a stolen ice-cream bicycle?

"It's not our fault," the policeman explained. "There are very few of us and lots and lots of thieves. We do our best, but . . ." He shrugged his shoulders.

Uncle thanked the policeman

quietly. Then, with the two
boys following him, he left the
police station and they began
the long walk home.

Uncle went back to the police
station the next day. Misipo

waited eagerly to hear whether there was any news of the bicycle, but of course there was none. It was the same the following day, and the day after that. Then the policeman told Uncle that he should stop bothering them. If they ever found the bicycle, they would let him know.

"What will you do now?" Misipo asked his uncle. "Can you buy another bicycle?"

Uncle shook his head.

"I haven't got the money," he said. "I'll have to give up selling ice-creams. I think I can get a job on a building site. I've heard they're looking for men."

"I'll try and get a job myself," Misipo said. "Then I can save up the money to buy you a new bike."

Uncle smiled.

"That's kind of you," he

said. "But you have to go to school."

Misipo knew that this was true, but he was determined that one day he would make it up to his uncle. It might be many years before he could repay him, but he would do it eventually.

Chapter Three

Three weeks later, when
everyone had given up any
hope of getting the ice-cream
bicycle back, Sepo came
running to Misipo's house early
one morning. Misipo was still
in bed when he arrived, and he
wondered what had brought his
friend to see him at such an
hour.

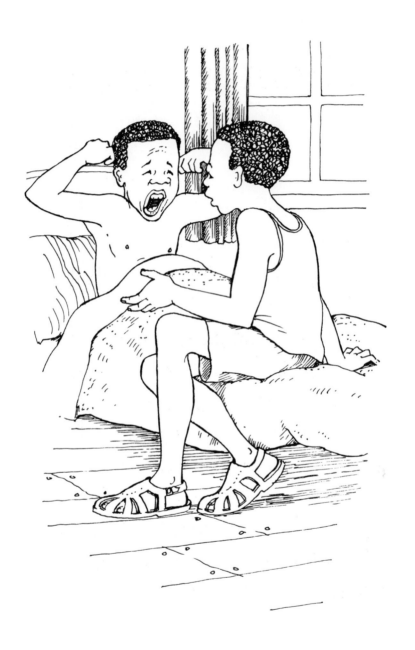

"I've got some important news," Sepo cried. "I think I've seen the ice-cream bicycle. I saw it last night."

Misipo caught his breath.

"Where?" he asked.

"It's quite far away," said Sepo. "In somebody's shed. I'm sure it's the one."

"Should we go to the police?" Misipo said. "Should we tell them?"

Sepo looked thoughtful.

"Yes," he said. "But only when we're certain. Why don't we go along together to look at it? Then, if you think it's the one, we can tell your uncle and he can call the police."

Misipo thought this was a good idea. Quickly he told his parents that he was going out with Sepo, and then, slipping into his shoes, he left the house with his friend. It was so early in the morning that there was hardly anyone about, but all over the town, in the backyards of the houses, cocks were beginning to crow and the first wisps of smoke were starting to drift up from the cooking fires.

As they made their way along the deserted roads, Sepo told Misipo of how he had seen the bicycle. He had taken an unusual route home the evening before when suddenly the ice-cream bicycle shot right past him.

"I could hardly believe it," Sepo said. "I stood quite still, and then the bicycle turned off the road in front of me and went into somebody's yard. I saw a man get off it and put it

in a shelter beside the house.
Then he covered it with sacking
and went inside."

When they reached the house,
the two boys crept round the
hedge that ran along the side

until they were as close as they could get to the shelter. Just as Sepo had said, there was a pile of sacking, and underneath it there was something which looked exactly the shape of the ice-cream bicycle.

"There's nobody about," Misipo whispered. "Let's creep in and take a look."

As quietly as they could, Sepo and Misipo slipped through the hedge and darted across the open ground that lay between them and the shelter. Then, raising the corner of the heavy sacking, they peered underneath.

There was the white box over the front wheel. There was the great silver bell on the handlebars. There was the dent which had been caused by a car which had scraped the side of the box a few months ago. There it was – the ice-cream bicycle!

Suddenly a dog began to bark. Misipo dropped the sacking and spun round. He looked at Sepo, who was pointing towards the house.

"It's inside," he whispered. "It must have heard us."

The dog was now barking furiously, scraping at the door.

Then there came the sound of somebody calling out.

"Quick," hissed Misipo. "We must get out of here."

The boys lost no time in running from the shelter, but even before they had reached the hedge, the door of the house burst open and a tall man wearing brown overalls emerged.

"You!" he shouted. "You boys! You stop right there!"

The two boys did not dare to look back. Throwing themselves to the ground, they wriggled their way under the hedge and out on to the road.

"I saw you!" the man called out, running towards the hedge. "If you come back here, I'll set my dog on you!"

The boys were soon well away from the house, panting from the effort of their run. After they had caught their breath, they quickly made their way back to Misipo's house to pass on to Uncle the news of what they had found.

"Are you sure it's my bicycle?" Uncle asked.

"Yes," said Misipo emphatically. "It was the ice-cream bicycle."

"We'll get the police," said Uncle. "You'll have to show them the place."

"That won't be hard," said Sepo.

"Then let's waste no time," said Uncle.

At the police station they saw the policeman to whom they had first reported the theft.

"I'm very busy," he said. "So I hope that this really is the bicycle."

"It is," said Misipo. "I would never mistake that bicycle."

This time they walked boldly up to the front of the house.

"There it is," said Misipo

proudly, pointing to the sacking. "The ice-cream bicycle is under that."

The policeman glanced at the sacking as he knocked on the door of the house. After a few moments the door opened and the tall man looked out. It was the same man the boys had seen earlier on, but he gave no sign of recognizing them.

"What do you keep under that sacking?" the policeman asked. "Will you please show it to us?"

"Why?" said the man defiantly. "This is my yard."

The policeman began to look
angry.

"I believe you have a stolen
bicycle there," he said.

"What?" exploded the man.
"A stolen bicycle? That there is
my own delivery bicycle.
That's all."

"Then prove it," said Uncle.
"Show it to us."

The man cast an angry
glance at Uncle and came out
of the house. Without saying
anything, he led them to the
pile of sacking and pulled it
off. There was a bicycle
underneath – a grocery
delivery bicycle, painted red,

with a large wire basket in the place where the ice-cream box would have been.

The policeman looked severely at the two boys. Then, turning to the man, he made an apology. "I'm sorry to have bothered you," he said.

"We weren't lying," Misipo protested to Uncle when they returned to the house. "We saw the ice-cream bicycle. I promise you."

"But it wasn't the ice-cream bicycle," Uncle said. "You must have imagined it."

"I didn't imagine it," Misipo

insisted. "It was there. I saw it. Sepo saw it too."

"Well," said Uncle. "It isn't there now, is it?"

Misipo did not know what to say. He was certain he had found the bicycle thief, and he was now more determined than ever to find the ice-cream bicycle itself.

Chapter Four

The more Misipo thought about it, the more certain he became.

"I know what must have happened," he said to Sepo. "When that man saw us, he must have suspected that we were looking at the bicycle. And because it was stolen, he would have had to move it.

Just in case."

Sepo nodded.

"That means he must have hidden it somewhere and put that red bicycle in its place."

"Yes," said Misipo. "So if we watched him for a while, we might find out where he's hidden the ice-cream bicycle. It

must be somewhere close to his house, as he wouldn't have had time to hide it otherwise."

Sepo agreed that this was a good idea.

"When shall we do it?" he asked.

"Tomorrow," said Misipo. "We'll hide near the hedge and

wait until he goes out."

"It could take hours," said Sepo. "It could take all day."

"That doesn't matter," said Misipo. "We can wait."

It was not difficult for the two boys to find themselves a hiding-place near the house. It was rather uncomfortable, being curled up under a bush, but it was impossible for anybody to see them there and they had a very good view of the front of the tall man's house.

Hours passed. Other people came out of their houses and

walked down the road. One or two people rode by on bicycles. A rubbish van moved slowly past. But in the house itself there was no movement.

By the time afternoon came, the two boys felt cramped and uncomfortable. Both of them were hot and thirsty and Misipo was just on the point of giving up when Sepo touched his arm.

"Look," he whispered. "He's coming out."

Misipo watched as the tall man stepped out of the house and locked the door behind him. Then, with his hands in his pockets, the man strolled out of the gate and began to make his way down the road.

"Wait until he's gone a little bit further," said Misipo. "Then we can start to follow him."

The two boys kept well back as the tall man walked on. At last, coming to a rather run-down house standing in a large yard, he walked up to the door and knocked. The boys watched as he was admitted to

the house and the door closed
behind him.

"What now?" asked Sepo.
"Do you think this is the
place?"

"It could be," said Misipo.
"Let's look."

Taking great care not to be
seen from inside the house, the
two boys sneaked into the
yard. There was a shed at the
back, and this was where
Misipo wanted to look. To
reach it without being seen,
though, they would have to
crawl past the window on their
stomachs – just like snakes.

It was a slow business, but at

last they reached their goal.
Pushing open the door, they
slipped into the dark shed and
looked about them. Inside, it
was almost empty. All they
could see was a few boxes, a
spade, and . . . the ice-cream
bicycle.

"Let's go to the police," said
Sepo. "We'll show them we

weren't wrong in the first place."

"No," whispered Misipo.
"The police probably wouldn't
come. Not after we were wrong
the last time."

"Well, what can we do?"
Sepo asked. "We can't just
forget about it."

Misipo did not answer. He

was too busy wheeling the ice-
cream bicycle round so that it
faced the door of the shed.
Then he gave his reply.

"We're taking it home," he
said. "When I give the signal,
throw open the door. Then
jump up on the top of the box
and I'll pedal."

Sepo swallowed hard. They would certainly be seen, and they would just as certainly be chased. Would they get away? He was not at all sure.

Chapter Five

When Misipo gave the signal,
Sepo flung open the door of the
shed and clambered up on to
the top of the box. Then, with
Misipo struggling to reach the
pedals, they wobbled their way
out of the shed towards the
gate.

As they passed the front of

the house there was the sound of shouting from inside. By the time they reached the gate, the door had opened and two men, the tall man and another one, had come out and begun to run after them.

"Thieves!" cried the tall man. "Stop those boys! Thieves!"

One or two people in the road looked round in surprise. One man was on a bicycle and he stopped immediately. The tall man called out to him.

"Catch those boys," he yelled. "They've stolen my bicycle."

The man remounted and
began to cycle after them,
shouting out as he did so.

"Quicker," urged Sepo,
seeing the other bicycle begin
to catch up with them.

"I can't go any quicker,"
panted Misipo. "This bicycle's
far too heavy." No matter how

hard he pedalled, he could not
seem to make the ice-cream
bicycle go any faster. The road
began to slope downhill a little
now, and that helped, but it
also helped the other bicycle,
which was now only a few
yards behind them. Misipo shot
a glance over his shoulder and
saw the man struggling behind
them. And running behind

71

him, not all that far away,
were the tall man and his
friend.

Suddenly Sepo called out,
"Watch where you're going!"

It was too late. Misipo had
been looking behind him and
so had not seen the road
turning. With an awful lurch

the ice-cream bicycle left the
road and careered down a
grassy bank. Misipo applied
the brakes, hoping to stop the
bicycle in its headlong flight,
but they had little effect.

At the bottom of the bank
there was a hedge. It was not a
thick hedge and it was not

strong enough to stop the ice-
cream bicycle shooting through
it like a bullet. Fortunately, on
the other side, there was a flat
piece of ground. By some
miracle Misipo had been able
to keep in the saddle on the
bumpy ride down and Sepo,
though he almost fell off at one

or two points, had also clung on to his uncomfortable perch. Now Misipo applied the brakes again, and this time they worked. The ice-cream bicycle came to a halt and, very slowly and very gently, toppled over.

The two boys picked themselves up and brushed the dust off their clothes. Then they inspected the bicycle and saw that it, too, was undamaged.

"We made it!" Misipo said to Sepo. "We got away!"

As he spoke, he realized that a man had emerged from a building near by and was

standing over them, looking rather cross.

"And what about our hedge?" he asked. "Can you please explain that?"

Misipo looked up and gasped. The man was a policeman and was clearly angry that two boys had made such a messy entrance to the back of a police station.

It did not take long before everything was sorted out. While Misipo stayed at the police station, Sepo was allowed to run off to fetch Uncle. When he arrived, he

could hardly believe that his
bicycle had been found. He
inspected it closely and was
reassured that this time there
was no mistake. Then, when
everything had been written
down by the policeman, Uncle
was permitted to wheel his
bicycle out on to the road.

"Let's go home now," said Misipo. "I feel very hungry."

Uncle, who was beaming with pleasure, shook his head.

"No," he said. "We three have work to do."

Seeing the two boys look puzzled, Uncle explained.

"There's still time to go to

the factory and pick up a load of ice-creams," he said. "And I should think that a large ice-cream would satisfy your hunger, wouldn't it?"

Misipo smiled, and then looked at Sepo. Sepo nodded.

"Yes," said Misipo, speaking for both of them. "Yes, Uncle, it would!"